MATTESON PUBLIC LIBRARY

3 1486 00267 7247

W9-CBR-422

Matteson Public Library

801 S. School Ave.

Matteson, IL 60443

Ph: 708-748-4431

www.mattesonpubliclibrary.org

DEMCO

For Julia and Mason—
with sprinkles
—T. S.

For Mom,
who let me be me
—S. M.

SIMON & SCHUSTER BOOKS FOR YOUNG READERS • An imprint of Simon & Schuster Children's Publishing Division • 1230 Avenue of the Americas, New York, New York 10020 • Text copyright © 2010 by Tammi Sauer • Illustrations copyright © 2010 by Scott Magoon • All rights reserved, including the right of reproduction in whole or in part in any form. • SIMON & SCHUSTER BOOKS FOR YOUNG READERS is a trademark of Simon & Schuster, Inc. • For information about special discounts for bulk purchases, please contact Simon & Schuster Special Sales at 1-866-506-1949 or business@simonandschuster.com. • The Simon & Schuster Speakers Bureau can bring authors to your live event. For more information or to book an event, contact the Simon & Schuster Speakers Bureau at 1-866-248-3049 or visit our website at www.simonspeakers.com. • Book design by Lizzy Bromley • The text for this book is set in Clichee. • The illustrations for this book are rendered digitally. • Manufactured in China • 0110 SCP • 10 9 8 7 6 5 4 3 2 1 • Library of Congress Cataloging-in-Publication Data • Sauer, Tammi. • Mostly monsterly / Tammi Sauer ; illustrated by Scott Magoon.—1st ed. • p. cm. • "A Paula Wiseman Book." • Summary: On the outside, Bernadette is a lot like the other monsters in her class but when she shows that she can be sweet, her classmates reject her until she finds a way to fit in again. • ISBN 978-1-4169-6110-9 (hardcover) • [1. Monsters—Fiction. 2. Individuality—Fiction. 3. Schools—Fiction.] • I. Magoon, Scott, ill. II. Title. • PZ7.S2502Mos 2010 • [E]—dc22 • 2008048676

first edition

MOSTLY MONSTERLY

TAMMI SAUER

Illustrated by SCOTT MAGOON

MATTESON PUBLIC LIBRARY

A PAULA WISEMAN BOOK
Simon & Schuster Books for Young Readers
New York London Toronto Sydney

On the outside Bernadette was mostly monsterly.

POINTY EARS

HUGE EYES

FANGS

CLAWS

CREEPY NECKLACE

TAIL

TWO TOES

She lurched.

She growled.

She caused
mayhem of all kinds.

But underneath the fangs and fur, Bernadette had a deep . . .
dark . . . secret. Sometimes, when she was all by herself,

she liked to pick flowers.

And pet kittens.

MILK

And *bake.*

For a monster
Bernadette was just
a little too sweet.

When it came time to go to school with the other monsters,
Bernadette felt a teensy bit nervous . . .

In Monster Moves Class, everyone practiced lurching techniques.

Except Bernadette.

"Group hug, everybody!"

That didn't go over so well.

During Creepy Noises Class, everyone worked on growling skills.

Except Bernadette.

She burst into song.

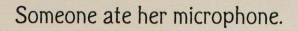
Someone ate her microphone.

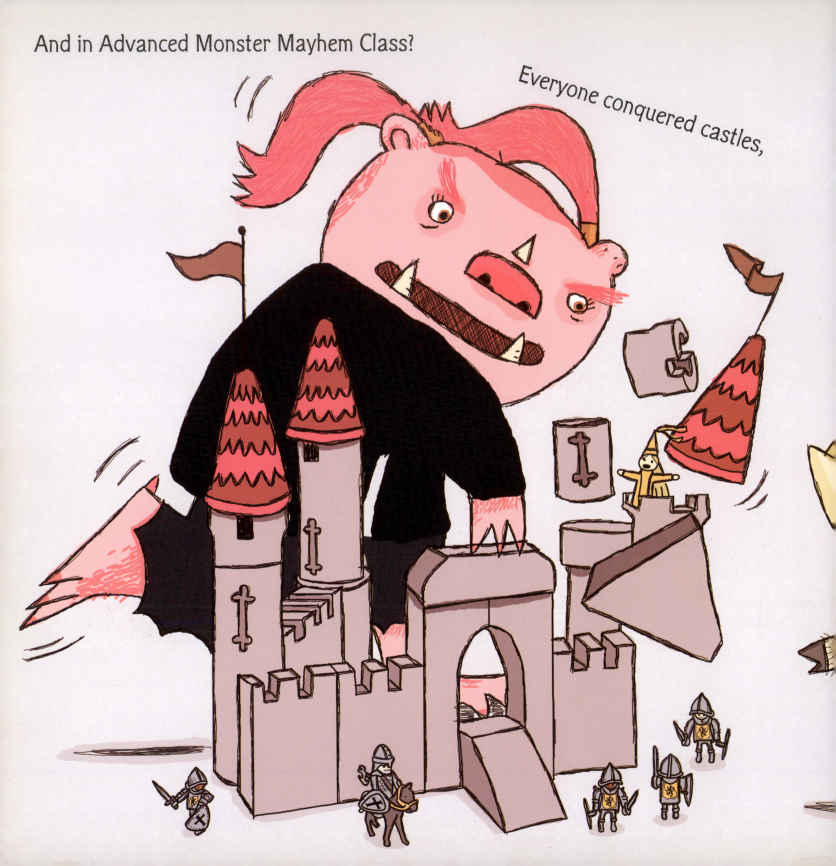

And in Advanced Monster Mayhem Class?

Everyone conquered castles,

dismantled villages,

and flattened cities.

Except you-know-who.

The other monsters gaped.

Clearly, this situation called for Bernadette's Secret Weapon . . .

"Treats!"

Bernadette's classmates crowded around her and smacked their lips.

"Bug parts?"
Bernadette shook her head.

"Fried snail goo?"
"Nope." said Bernadette.

"Fish heads dipped in hot sauce?!"
"Even better."

She lifted the lid.

"CUPCAKES WITH SPRINKLES!"

"Gross!"
The other monsters took one look, then huffed out to recess.

Bernadette's tail drooped.

She trudged to the window and watched her classmates on the playground.
They stomped. They slobbered. They scared the leaves off the trees.

"They're acting like total monsters," said Bernadette.

"Wait!" A toothy grin spread across her face.

"That's it!"

Bernadette went right to work.

After recess the monsters eyeballed their desks.
"Ew," they grumbled.
"Those cards are probably *nice*."

Then they took a closer look.

Soon everyone got in the spirit of things.

As for Bernadette...

"Group hug?"

She earned herself a gold star.

Bernadette was mostly monsterly.

She lurched.

She growled.

She caused mayhem of all kinds.

But sometimes . . .

She was just Bernadette.
And that was okay too.